Frazzled

and

Frumpy

Super Mum book two

Stacey Broadbent

Published by Stacey Broadbent
Copyright © 2021 Stacey Broadbent

Second edition

Originally published as Super Mum! Frazzled, Frumpy and Fabulous! 2016

Licence Notes

This is a work of fiction. Names, characters, places and incidents are used fictitiously. Any resemblance to actual persons, living or dead, events or locales is entirely coincidental.

Proofreading by Spell Bound
Cover design by Stacey Broadbent
Cover images from Deposit Photos

ISBN: 978-0-473-57172-6 (paperback)
        978-0-473-57173-3 (MOBI)

For all those mothers who are at their wits end, feeling underappreciated.

In case no one has told you today, and you're feeling invisible—
I see you.
You are the fixer of boo-boos, the reader of bedtime stories, and the loving arms that hold your family together.

You are doing the best that you can and don't let anyone tell you different.
You are fabulous!

Contents

Calamity Jayne

Well, that's definitely a contender for the 'nailed it' file," I huff as I wipe my sticky fingers down the front of my apron, leaving a smear of raspberry jam and purple food colouring.

"It's not that bad," hubby says, trying to stifle a laugh. "I think it has character."

I stare at him with one eyebrow cocked. "Are we looking at the same cake?" I ask, pointing at the monstrosity in front of me. "The big purple square with a hole in the middle and Minnie Mouse stacked precariously in said hole?"

He breaks, a deep chuckle erupting. "Babe, she's only turning four, and she's our daughter, not Gordon Ramsey. She's going to love it!"

"It doesn't even look remotely like a car!" I throw my hands up in frustration. "She asked for Minnie Mouse in a car. The pictures on Pinterest made it look so easy!" I grumble, folding my arms across my chest like a petulant child. "The stupid doll is bigger than I realised, so I had to cut a bigger hole—then I couldn't shape it properly, otherwise it would fall apart. And I rolled the icing too thin, so you can see the jam underneath, which I tried to cover with lollies, but clearly, they do *not* want to play the game and keep falling off! This is my biggest birthday cake disaster since the fluorescent orange Pooh Bear fiasco of '04!"

"Hey! I liked Pooh Bear." He pauses, his brow furrowed as if in deep thought. "You really think that one was worse than the Picasso cat of 2011?"

"Oh God, I completely forgot about that one! That was pretty bad."

He chuckles. "I was joking! You're being too hard on yourself. All Zoe will care about is that it's a cake with lollies and Minnie Mouse. Who cares if it looks like a purple box is eating Minnie?" He grins playfully. I open my mouth to retort, but he stops me with a kiss. Taking a hold of my shoulders, he says, "Now, put down the spatula, and go put your feet up. You look exhausted."

"Gee thanks. You always know just what to say." I roll my eyes but allow him to lead me over to the couch anyway. He pulls a bean bag in front of me and sits down. Grabbing hold of my ankle, he pulls my sock off and rests it on his lap as he slowly starts kneading my foot.

"Mmmm, God that feels good," I say, throwing my head back and closing my eyes, my hands resting on my protruding belly. Eight months in and my skin is already stretched to capacity. I've got little red and purple lines forming the weirdest crossword puzzle I've ever seen across my belly to prove it. Three big babies, and still my skin needs to stretch even further! Don't ask me how that's even possible.

Frazzled and Frumpy

Hubby continues to massage my feet, and they slowly begin to feel somewhat normal again—well, as normal as they can be in my pregnant state. My feet seem to have taken to retaining fluid and have swollen so much that I can't even squeeze them into jandals. I am quite literally barefoot and pregnant.

This has become our nightly ritual of late. I make some kind of disastrous concoction in the kitchen, and hubby placates me while relieving my aching feet.

I blame my sister, Tegan. It had been her suggestion that I start writing a food blog in the first place, as a way to make some extra cash. I had been sceptical at first, but her enthusiasm eventually rubbed off on me, and I leapt forth into the world of food blogging.

She helped me come up with the name; *Calamity Jayne, my hit and miss guide to being a foodie.* I like to think of myself as a rather good cook, but there are always those catastrophes that happen—that's where the calamity part comes in. My very first blog post was a retelling of the events leading up to her birthday.

I didn't have a lot of money at the time and decided to make her some hot-chocolate truffles that I'd seen on Pinterest (note the pattern here). This is what happened:

The first part was easy – melt the chocolate and cream together and leave it to cool in the fridge—got it.

The second part, also easy. Place blobs of mix onto wax paper, then place back into the fridge—got it.

Frazzled and Frumpy

Now the next part—roll mix into balls and wrap in cling film—sounds like it should've been super simple, but alas, this was not the case. Firstly, the chocolate mix did not want to come off the paper (I used greaseproof paper, which I assumed was the same thing—but I'm thinking maybe I was mistaken), so I ended up scraping it off and blobbing it onto the cling film—leaving a lot of chocolate behind and covering myself in it also (not such a bad thing). I decided that perhaps the freezer would be the best place to leave them to turn into 'truffles' as they were meant to be.

The next morning, I went to the freezer to collect the truffles and see if I could shape them into ball shapes rather than blobs. To my dismay, I discovered the truffles were *still* squishy, and no amount of shaping was going to work. Seeing as they didn't look aesthetically pleasing, I figured I should probably try one and make sure they at least tasted as they should— a little quality control, if you will. So, I got my mug of milk and pulled out a white chocolate truffle. I slowly eased it open, only to discover the truffle had stuck to the cling film too. Palm, meet face.

I then tried to scoop the mix off the cling film and into my mug (again leaving chocolate behind!). Sighing, I figured I may as well continue scraping—I mean, I couldn't waste any more chocolate! That would be sacrilege!

Okay, so they may not have *looked* as they should, but they tasted amazing!

Frazzled and Frumpy

Anywho, after the truffle debacle, I decided to make some cupcakes to accompany those wonderfully unattractive, yet tasty, balls of chocolatey goodness.

While those were cooking, I started on the decorations. Yeah, that's right, I attempted to make decorations out of fondant. I had watched a demo at the local culinary supplies store a few weeks back and thought it looked easy. I mean, how hard could it be?

How hard indeed! My childhood days were spent forming roses out of clay, and yet I couldn't seem to get the fondant to do what I wanted it to. The roses ended up as unappealing, flat-leaved flowers (if you can call them that) that would stick to everything they came into contact with.

Needless to say, I gave up on roses and made a couple of pigs (Tegan's suggestion—that's right, I wasn't finished by the time she came around—birthday presents nailed!). First pig stuck to the board—this really was not my day! It was then that I remembered seeing them use a plastic bag at the store, so I gave that a go. Thankfully, it did the trick. Winning!

Once the cupcakes had cooled and were ready for icing, I made an awesome chocolate buttercream (if I do say so myself), grabbed my new icing tip, scooped the icing into the bag, and started to decorate...

Bag burst.

Dammit!

And that was how my venture into food blogging began. One giant disaster!

Frazzled and Frumpy

I had been so sure that the Minnie Mouse cake would be my redeeming post. Something I could be proud of.

It seems the name Calamity Jayne is even more apt that I first thought.

A Birthday Surprise

I wake to the happiest sound in the world; my daughter singing.

"No more sleeps to go! No more sleeps till my birthday! It's my birthday!"

Hubby rolls over to face me. "I guess she's awake then." He chuckles as he slides across the bed to give me a quick cuddle before the birthday celebrations begin. I can already hear the girls climbing out of bed, the pitter-patter of their footsteps echoing off the wooden floors.

"It's my birthday!" Zoe announces loudly as she bounds onto our bed.

"Is it? Are you sure?" I ask, grinning at her. "I think it's my birthday, not yours."

She giggles. "No, Mummy! You're silly! It's my birthday! Remember? I'm turning this many." She slowly counts her fingers, her tongue sticking out for concentration. "This many!" She holds four fingers up proudly.

"Wow! Are you four now?" I ask, feigning shock. She nods enthusiastically.

"Uh-huh."

"Can we give her presents now?" Ellie asks, bouncing on our bed.

Frazzled and Frumpy

"Woah there, Tiger. If you keep bouncing like that, you'll bounce us all off the bed," hubby says, pulling himself up to a sitting position. "Anyway, we can't do the presents until your brother is up."

"I'll go wake him!" She takes off before we can stop her.

"I'll be back in a minute. Don't start without me," I say, rolling myself out of bed. I swear this baby thinks my bladder is a trampoline. Donning my pink bathrobe, I pad to the bathroom.

I finish up and head back through the kitchen, checking the cake is still intact and secretly hoping that the kitchen fairies have come and fixed my poor excuse for a birthday cake. To my disappointment, the purple eyesore is still in one piece. It hasn't magically transformed as I'd hoped.

I have been trying unsuccessfully to make the perfect cake since Devon was a baby. He's going to be fourteen this year, and I'm still yet to reach that goal. Sure, some of them have been good, but not *Oh My God* great, you know? The one they have loved the most, that has been requested the most, is a simple pizza cake. A flat sponge cake decorated with jam (sauce), lollies (toppings), and icing drizzles (cheese). There's something to be said about simplicity, I guess. It's so easy I could do it with my eyes closed.

A dramatic sigh from the bedroom draws my attention back to the present, and I make my way back to my family, one hand resting on my lower back, the other on my belly. All three children are perched on the bed now, waiting for my return.

Frazzled and Frumpy

"Mum! You took for ages!" Zoe says, throwing her hands in the air.

"I'm so sorry, my darling. It's not easy to manoeuvre this here belly," I say, rubbing my hand across my stomach.

Zoe reaches out, placing her hands on either side of my waist. She licks her lips and kisses my belly button, leaving her lips pressed against me. "Morning, baby. It's my birthday!"

The baby responds to her voice, rolling from one side to the other, making Zoe giggle.

"I think baby is saying happy birthday to you," I say, grinning. "Hmmm, now, where did I put those presents?" I tap my fingers across my chin. "Where, where, where…"

Zoe giggles and claps her hands.

"Maybe they're in here," I say, checking behind the mirror.

"No, Mummy! They wouldn't fit there!" Zoe laughs.

"No? Hmmm. Maybe in here." I walk over to the cupboard, easing it open a fraction and peeking inside. I look back over my shoulder at the children. "I think there's a present in here," I whisper.

"Yay!" Ellie and Zoe cry out in unison. Even Devon has a grin on his face.

"Ta-da!" I pull out a couple of parcels. "Look what I found!"

"Presents!"

Zoe stares at them with a look of pure joy on her face. "Can I open them?" she asks. Any other child would just dive straight in, but not my Zoe. Don't ask me why. Normally she is a right little terror, giving me more than my fair share of grey hairs. But put a present in front of her, and she turns into this polite little angel.

"Of course you can," I say, setting them down beside her. She gently runs a finger along the top of each one, as if deciding which one to give her attention to. Finally, she settles on the smallest one first. She carefully peels the Sellotape from each section and eases the paper open.

"Oh! It's a book!" she cries. "Thank you!" She turns it over in her hands, looking at the pictures.

"There's a CD in there too, so you can listen to the story."

"Really? I always wanted one like that!" she exclaims. See? Perfect little angel.

She goes through this process with each gift. Each one gets a surprised "Oh!" and a gushed "Thank you!"

With the presents all opened, I send the children to their bedrooms to dress for the day while I prepare the birthday breakfast; pancakes with bacon and maple syrup. Zoe is a bacon fiend, and when I stumbled across a fun looking recipe that incorporated two of her favourite foods, I knew I had to make it for her. I heated the pan, adding a few small slices of streaky bacon. While they cooked, I got to whisking up the batter. I flipped each strip of bacon onto the other side, and carefully spooned the batter over each piece. It was supposed to look like perfectly rounded, fluffy pancakes, with bacon in the centre. My batter was perhaps a little too runny and wouldn't circle the bacon. It kept running along the side of the pan, the result being strips of pancake attached to strips of bacon.

Close enough.

I set the plates on the table. "Pancakes are ready!" I call out, pouring a dollop of maple syrup over the top of each plate.

"Pancakes!" Ellie yells as she skips to the table.

"Pancakes!" Zoe echoes. She clambers onto her seat and peers at her plate. "What's that?" she asks, her brows pulled into a frown.

"Pancakes with bacon, just like you asked."

"That's not pancakes," she says, pushing the food around with her fork.

"It is, it just looks different. Taste it. You'll see."

She gives me a sceptical look but takes a nibble of the piece on her fork. "Mmmmm, pancakes!" She grins before shovelling a forkful into her mouth. I breathe a sigh of relief.

"Are you taking a picture for the blog?" hubby asks, patting my bottom on the way past.

"Another epic fail post, you reckon?" I ask.

"I wouldn't say that. They taste great. You just need to work on your presentation," he says, mimicking one of those celebrity judges on a cooking show.

"It probably would make a good blog post, I guess. 'Fugly food you'll love'." I make finger quotes in the air. Hubby chokes out a laugh. "You like that, huh?"

"Sounds perfect." He kisses my forehead before swiping another pancake for his plate.

Frazzled and Frumpy

The guests have all arrived, and I'm busy flitting about in the kitchen, putting the final touches onto the party food. Hubby has been making coffees for all the adults, and Devon has been tasked with keeping the younger kids occupied. He is taking them through a game of musical chairs at the moment, and all I can hear are squeals of laughter. It makes my heart sing.

"Want any help?" Tegan asks, wrapping her arms around my middle as far as she can. I pat her hands and lean my head back to meet hers.

"Thanks, that would be great. Can you help me bring these plates out?" I point at the selection of platters covering my benches. I don't know how it happens. Every single time we throw any kind of gathering, I go into panic mode. "Have I got enough food? Do you think I need to make more?" I always end up with my benches being laden with leftovers that last us a few days. It's better to have too much, than not enough, though, I guess.

She grabs the savouries and sandwiches, and I take the cocktail sausages and fairy bread. We weave our way through the throngs of people and place them on the table.

Frazzled and Frumpy

"Grubs up!" she yells, her hand cupped around her mouth.

I waddle back to the kitchen to retrieve a bowl of lollies and some chips. Sis is busy pouring cups of lemonade for the kids, while I usher the rest to the table to eat.

I help them to get a selection of food on their napkins and bring it over to the smaller table for them to sit at. The adults hover about, picking at the food as they pass by.

"You should sit down, have a break," hubby says as he hands me a much-needed cup of tea.

"Thanks, I will. I just want to make sure everyone has something to eat."

"I can do that. Sit down, give your feet a rest." I smile at him as he helps me to the couch. It would be nice to relax for a few minutes. Birthday parties can be rather draining!

The children are too hyped up to sit still for long. They scatter, leaving half-eaten food in their wake. At least they are easy to entertain at this age. Devon gets them started on a game of tag, while hubby retrieves what's needed for pass-the-parcel.

I feel lazy watching them do all the work. Birthday parties have always been my domain, but they refuse to let me do anything. Instead, I settle in, my feet folded beneath me and my belly resting in my lap. I know it won't be long before my legs begin to tingle from the extra weight on them, but I don't care. At this point in the pregnancy it's nigh on impossible to find a comfortable position for any length of time.

Frazzled and Frumpy

As the children are gathering for the next game, I realise Zoe isn't with them. I quickly scan the room, and go to stand up to search for her, when hubby's father comes through from the kitchen, a grin on his face.

"You missing someone?" he asks.

"Yeah, Zoe. Have you seen her?"

"Uh, yeah. I hope you got a picture of that cake already."

"What? Why?"

"Go and have a look in the kitchen." He moves aside, allowing me room to waddle past. I am completely unprepared for the sight that beholds me.

The pantry cupboard is wedged open, and tucked in between the shelves and the door, is Zoe. With the cake. On the floor. She's eating it.

"Zoe!" I exclaim, unsure whether to laugh or cry. It hadn't been my best work, but I'd worked damn hard on that cake all the same.

She grins up at me, a half-eaten lolly hanging from her lips. "I love my cake, Mum!" she squeals in delight. I crouch down to see how much damage has been done. Surprisingly, the cake is still intact and mostly on the chopping board. Mostly. Somehow, she managed to pull the entire thing down from the shelf and onto the floor. If I'm honest, I'm actually impressed. That cake weighed a tonne!

I scoop the board up and place it on the bench. Now what? They'll all be expecting cake. I can't serve floor cake, can I?

Frazzled and Frumpy

I look up at Tegan, who is standing in the doorway trying to suppress a giggle. "What do I do now?" I ask.

"They're kids! They won't care. Anyway, it didn't actually touch the floor, well, not much of it. Most of it stayed on the board, it's just had Zoe's fingers on it, and let's face it, what's a kids birthday cake without children's grubby fingerprints?" She grins at me.

"I guess... There *is* a lot of cake there. It would be a shame for it to be wasted."

"Yes. Yes, it would." She turns to the guests in the other room. "Who wants floor cake?" she asks loudly.

"Me!" the children all scream and come running. They gather around me, staring at the monstrosity I have created.

"Wow!"

"Cool! You're so lucky, Zoe!"

"Yum! I want that piece!"

They all start poking and prodding the cake, grabbing lollies from the sides as I stand by and watch. Sis wraps her arm around my shoulders. "See? Told ya."

I can't help but smile. Maybe it wasn't as bad as I thought.

~ 21 ~

Spending Spree

"What are you going to buy with your birthday money, honey?" I ask a very excited Zoe. She had been given a few envelopes with cash from grandparents, and I had promised her we would go shopping while the others were at school. Ellie had started a few months ago, and Zoe had calmed somewhat now that it was just the two of us at home.

"Ummm, maybe a doll? Or a colouring book! Or some bubbles! Or chocolate! Can I get chocolate, Mummy?" She jumps up and down with the biggest grin on her face, and I find myself caught up in her enthusiasm.

"Of course you can, darling. It's your money. How about we look at the toys first though?" I grab her hand and lead her across the carpark. She skips along happily, her purse clutched in her little fist.

The first thing we see upon entering the store, is a giant plush teddy bear. Right on cue, Zoe gushes, "Ooh a teddy! Can I buy it?" She pulls free from my grasp and runs straight for the display, diving into the big bear. She climbs onto its lap and strokes the faux fur.

"It's pretty cool, isn't it? I don't think you have enough money for it though, sweetheart."

Frazzled and Frumpy

"Please?" She peers up at me with her big puppy-dog eyes, and I feel myself caving. Shaking my head and averting my eyes, I try to coax her to the toy aisle.

"Come on, let's go and see what else there is." I start walking away, hoping she'll follow, but I don't hear anything behind me. I pause, pretending to look at something so I can see what she's doing. She has curled herself into a ball and turned her back to me, one arm wrapped around the bear's neck, the other caressing its belly. Stubborn much?

"Zoe, come on please," I say, pressing a hand to my lower back as I stretch.

"No," she says, burying herself even further into the toy.

"Zoe, you can't sit there all day. If you want to spend your money then you have to come with me now, otherwise we'll just go straight back home." I can feel my cheeks burning as I try not to lose my cool in public. Deep down, I know people really aren't paying attention to us, but when your child has a meltdown in public, you can't help but feel like everyone is watching how you handle the situation. Why do our children always want to challenge us in front of other people?

I muster my best stern voice. "Zoe, now."

She lifts her chin in defiance and turns even further away from me. I march over and grab a hold of her wrist, pulling her to her feet.

"I told you to come with me, but you didn't listen, so guess what? We're going home now." I start walking towards the door, but Zoe digs her heels in and refuses to move. She starts pulling her hand from my grip. She is surprisingly strong!

"Let me go!" she screams. "Let me go!"

Great, now I look like I'm trying to kidnap my own daughter. I crouch down as best as I can in my ballooned state and attempt to grab her other arm.

"Zoe, stop," I hiss. "You're being silly."

"Let me go!" Her face scrunches up, getting redder by the minute as she fights to pull away from me. I need to defuse the situation.

"Stop fighting me and listen."

"Let me go!"

"If I let you go, will you stop and listen?"

"Yes!" she yells, narrowing her eyes at me so all I can see is the black of her pupil. I let her go, nearly losing my balance in the process. I didn't realise how much effort it was taking to stop her from running away. I can feel my legs protesting at the position I've been holding, but all the experts say you need to get down to their level, so that's where I'm going to stay until this is resolved.

"I understand that you want that teddy bear, but you don't have enough money for it today. I know that sucks, but you have two options. We can leave the store and you can try and save some money to buy the bear, or we can go to the toy aisle and see if there is anything else you can get with the money you have now." She appears to be calming down enough to think about what I have suggested. "So, do you want to keep shopping, or would you rather go home?"

Frazzled and Frumpy

"I want to keep shopping," she says quietly, glancing back over her shoulder one last time at the teddy. "Maybe they have smaller ones." She grins, and just like that, we're back on track.

I waddle towards the toy aisle while she skips ahead of me. My legs are all tingly from squatting for so long. I have to keep stopping to shake them out and try to get the blood pumping again.

By the time I get there, Zoe is already running down each aisle, a trail of toys in her wake. She is giggling and touching everything she passes. You wouldn't think this was the same kid who was staring me down only a few minutes before.

"Have you found anything you want?" I ask, leaning my frame against one of the shelves as I catch my breath. Yes, I *am* that unfit.

"I want this!" She holds up a water gun and a tiara. I love how the teddy bear has disappeared from her mind already.

"Okay, let me see how much they are." I inspect the tags and see that she has enough to get them both. "Good choosing," I say. "You can afford to get both if you want."

"Yip! Can I get bubbles too?"

"You might have enough to get a small one."

She grins and takes off down the aisle to retrieve the bubbles she wants. "Can I get this one?" She waves it in my face.

"Yes, you can get that one too. That will be all your money. Is that definitely what you want?" I ask, and she nods.

Frazzled and Frumpy

"Ya-huh."

"Okay, let's go up to the counter then."

We traipse back to the front of the store and line up to make our purchases. Zoe bounces up and down excitedly.

When we get to the checkout, she places everything up on the counter and tells the cashier that it was her birthday and this is her birthday money. The cashier smiles and rings up her order.

"You have to give her your money now, sweetheart."

She tips her purse out on the counter. The cashier takes the money and puts it in the cash register before handing Zoe her receipt and bag of goodies. She accepts them but doesn't move away from the checkout, just stands there staring at the cashier with her hand out.

"Thank you, have a great day," the cashier says.

Zoe frowns, turning to face me. "She took all my money, Mum."

"That's what happens when you buy things sweetheart. You have to pay for them."

"But she took *all* of my money! She could have given some back!"

I chuckle. "Honey, I told you, you would be spending all of your money, remember?"

"But... but... she took *all* of it," she whispers loudly, glaring at the cashier. I smile sheepishly at her, mouthing the words "I'm sorry".

"Come on, Zoe. Maybe we could go to the park and blow some bubbles?" I suggest hopefully.

Frazzled and Frumpy

"Okay." She draws the word out, never taking her eyes away from the cashier. I place my hands on her shoulders and attempt to usher her towards the door. She reluctantly follows my lead, all the while glaring at the poor cashier. I'm half expecting her to do the universal "I'm watching you" gesture, it's *that* intense.

Instead, though, in true Zoe form, just as we reach the door, she sticks her tongue out, waggling her fingers above her head.

Kids can be so embarrassing.

Expectations

The next night, I'm sitting on the couch, a myriad of pillows propped behind me and my feet resting on one of those exercise balls, quietly rubbing my belly and thinking about the impending birth. Unlike the last pregnancy, I have been making sure to appreciate the beauty of carrying another life inside my body. That being said, I'm nearing that point where you just want it to hurry up so you can meet your little bundle of joy. To see what they will look like, if they'll have a head of hair or be a little bald eagle. The anticipation is one of the best parts I think.

One of my least favourite parts of pregnancy, is that the area where my calf usually tapers down to my ankles has swollen so much that we are lovingly referring to them as 'cankles'. Yes, I am retaining a lot of fluid, and, as my substitute midwife tells me, it is perfectly normal. She says I just need to elevate my feet and drink more water. I think if I drank any more water, I would sound like a waterbed every time I took a step!

Now, hubby and I have turned this (the 'cankles') into a form of nightly entertainment. We like to play "Whose thumb print will stay the longest?" It's great fun! We each take turns pushing our thumbs into my sausage legs and holding for a few seconds, then see

Frazzled and Frumpy

how long the indents stay there. We've even tried to see how many thumbprints we can get on there at any one time. It's the small things that keep a marriage alive.

My mind wanders back to the birth. We made the decision not to find out the sex of this baby, but I'm quietly confident it'll be a boy. It just *feels* like I'm carrying the same as I did with Devon; low and all out front. I've still got a few weeks to go, but I already feel like I'm stretched to capacity.

I will admit, I'm a little bit scared of how big this baby will be. They say that boys are normally bigger, and if this one *is* a boy, I could very well be split in two! All my babies have been... large. In fact, Devon was my smallest at 10lb 2oz, and they've gotten bigger each time. Zoe was 11lb and even though she was the easiest to birth, I still feel anxious. I don't know how much bigger I can handle. Things can only stretch so far!

Perhaps I should try eating less? I mean, I've really embraced the whole 'eating for two' notion. I know you're not actually meant to, but I love food, and I'll take any excuse to overindulge, and growing a life inside of you seems like the perfect one to me.

I consider this option as I stuff a handful of potato chips into my mouth.

What? You're going to begrudge a pregnant woman her cravings? You wouldn't do that, would you?

Yes, I will stoop to guilt trips. Please don't judge me.

Frazzled and Frumpy

I must've drifted off, because I wake up to the sound of hubby chuckling at something on TV. I surreptitiously wipe chip crumbs from my cleavage and drag my cumbersome body farther up on the couch, grunting as I do. Real smooth.

If hubby noticed that I'd fallen asleep (and let's face it, that's highly likely given I've turned into one of those mouth-breathers when I sleep), he doesn't show it. He keeps his eyes front and centre, though his hand snakes around to entwine with mine. Yep. He totally noticed.

"Ellie, don't!" comes from the bedroom. Hubby and I exchange glances. The children have been asleep for hours, so Zoe must be talking in her sleep again. "Ellie!"

"I'll go," I say, shuffling to the front of the couch. Hubby places his hand on my lower back and gives a gentle shove to help me get to my feet.

I pad into their room and find Ellie half hanging off the bed, her sheets tangled around her middle. I nudge her farther onto the bed and do my best to cover her up. Zoe stirs again, throwing an arm over her face. She must be having a bad dream. I gently slip her arm back under the blankets and stroke the side of her face to calm her; she always loved that as a baby. I bend down to kiss her squishy cheeks and as I do, I feel something wet trickle down my legs and onto the floor.

Could it be? Did my waters just break?!

I dash out to the lounge, a look of confusion on my face. Hubby eyes me suspiciously.

"Everything okay?" he asks.

"I… I think my water just broke," I stutter.

Hubby's face drains of all colour. "Isn't it too early for that?"

I chuckle, you'd think after three births he'd have gotten used to it by now. "Yeah, it's early, but I'm only a couple of weeks off my due date."

"Okay, well, what shall I do? Do you want me to call the midwife? Do you need me to call your mum?"

"Woah there! The contractions haven't even started. It'll be a few more hours yet. Calm down. Go make us a cup of tea, and I'll go and clean up a bit," I say. It's so cute how stressed out he gets.

I waddle out to the bathroom and close the door. Grabbing a wad of toilet paper, I get to work cleaning up the surprisingly small amount of liquid. Hmmm. Maybe the baby is blocking the rest from coming out?

Hubby knocks on the door. "You okay?" he asks.

"Umm, yeah, I think so."

"You don't sound so confident."

"There's normally a lot more than this. It normally gushes. But there doesn't appear to be any more coming out."

"Is that good or bad?"

Frazzled and Frumpy

I open the door. "I don't know. Every other time, the waters have made a lot more mess and the contractions have come with them. I don't even have a slight feeling of tightness."

Hubby quirks an eyebrow at me and shifts uncomfortably.

"What?" I ask.

"You don't think... I mean... It couldn't have been an 'accident'?" he says, holding his fingers up in air quotes.

"You think I peed myself?" I ask as if it's the most preposterous suggestion in the world. In reality, I know I have already done this three times this week while having sneezing fits, so it's really not that far off the mark.

"I mean, I don't know. I thought that could happen?" he asks. I can tell he doesn't want to be having this conversation, and who can blame him? Suggesting that a heavily pregnant and highly emotional woman has peed herself—he's braver than most.

He looks so uncomfortable that I can't be mad at him. "I guess there's a slim possibility that that could be the case," I offer.

We sit on the couch and wait patiently for any sign of contractions.

There are none.

Turns out he was right.

I peed myself.

I'm not gonna lie, it's pretty embarrassing to admit that, but this shit happens. I make a silent promise to myself to practice those Kegel exercises more frequently than the random one I've been doing every few weeks.

Thinking I'm in labour when I'm just peeing my pants… that's definitely up there as one of the most embarrassing things I've ever done.

Something Sweet

"Mum!"

I blink my eyes open. It's still dark.

"Mum!"

I fumble for my phone to see what time it is—3AM. Of course it is. I throw the sheets back and roll out of bed, stumbling blindly through the lounge.

"Mum!"

"Yeah, I'm coming!" I say in a loud whisper. There's nothing I love more than being woken up in the early hours of the morning by a screaming child. And why is it always me they call for? Do they not realise they have two parents?

"What's wrong?" I ask, peering through the door.

"I can't find my giraaaaaaaaffe!" Zoe wails as if it's the end of the world. I stagger in, dodging the minefield of discarded toys. As I suspected, giraffe is lying on the floor right beside her bed. Didn't look very hard, did she? No, of course not. Why would she when she can holler for me to retrieve it for her?

I throw it on the bed and give her a quick kiss. "There, now go back to sleep. It's still sleepy time," I say.

I pad back to the bedroom, climb into bed, snuggle down under the blankets, and close my eyes.

Frazzled and Frumpy

And blink them back open again.

Great. That small trek to the girls' room was enough to wake up my tiny pregnancy bladder. I adjust my position and close my eyes again, hoping the feeling will subside but deep down knowing it won't. My mind won't let me forget it anyway. That little niggly feeling combined with my getting up was enough to stir my brain into awake mode, and now my thoughts are going a mile a minute. The constant song "Gotta pee, gotta pee, gotta pee pee pee," playing on a loop in the background in my mind.

I give in, swing my legs back out of bed and make my way to the bathroom.

Now I am wide awake, and sleep is not going to happen. I switch the jug on and go back to the bedroom to retrieve my dressing gown and book. May as well make the most of this uninterrupted child-free time.

Cup of tea in hand, I traipse back to the lounge and settle on the couch. Luckily, hubby bought me a book light for Christmas, and I can put it to good use now so as not to wake the children.

I have only read a paragraph before I hear stirring in the girls' room. A tiny whimper, followed by a sniff.

"Zoe?" I say softly. The unmistakable thud of a child jumping out of bed greets me. She comes bounding out to the lounge, giraffe clasped firmly in her hands. She leaps onto the couch and buries her face into my chest. I wrap my arm around her.

"What's wrong?" I ask.

"I'm scared of the dark," she whispers, her little body shaking.

Frazzled and Frumpy

"You know what? You're supposed to have your eyes closed when you sleep—that way you can't see that it's dark."

"But it's too dark to go to sleep," she says, lifting her head to look at me with her beautiful hazel eyes.

"What if I turn on the hall light? Do you think you could sleep then?"

She nods, climbing off the couch. I take her hand and lead her back to bed, switching the light on as we go past. I tuck her in and wipe the hair from her face. There's something so angelic about children when it's late at night and they're all sleepy. Somehow, they become just that little bit cuter, squishier, and more adorable. I kiss her cheek and tell her I love her.

"I love you too, Mummy."

"Honey." A hand rests on my shoulder, gently shaking me.

"Mmmm," I groan.

"You fell asleep on the couch. You should go back to bed," hubby says quietly.

I open one eye and peer up at him. "What time is it?" I mumble, struggling to straighten my body that is now stiff from resting in this awkward position. How on earth I fell asleep like this is beyond me. My neck is aching and one of my arms has got pins and needles.

"It's just after six. The kids are still asleep, so why don't you head back to bed for a bit?"

I attempt to nod, but my neck won't co-operate. Hubby chuckles and offers me his arm. He lifts me off the couch and leads me back to the bedroom.

We don't even make it through the door before the pitter-patter of feet can be heard. I muster a giggle. "Figures," I say, turning to them, my one good arm flinging out to the side to invite them in for a hug. "Good morning!" I sing.

"Daddy!" Ellie cries out, throwing herself into his arms.

What am I? Chopped liver?

When they need something done, it's "Mum!" but when they want cuddles, its "Dad!" I think I got the short end of the stick.

Admittedly, my protruding belly is right at head height for them, so I guess I'm not as cuddly as I used to be. I lower myself into one of the chairs at the table and hold my arm out again—the other one is slowly getting feeling back. This time they come running. I love those early-morning cuddles. It's such a great way to start the day.

"Just a little bit longer," I whisper into Ellie's ear as she starts to pull away. She giggles and wraps her arms around me even tighter.

"Like this?" she asks.

"Exactly like that."

Frazzled and Frumpy

We carry on with our morning. Ellie and Devon have school and Zoe is at home with me again. I busy myself making lunches, brushing hair and making sure that shoes are on the right feet. It really amazes me that they can walk around all day with their shoes on wrong. Is that not uncomfortable?

Anyways, we drop Ellie and Devon off and head back home. Zoe and I have plans to do some baking and then I think I'll let her watch a movie so I can get back to that book I was reading.

We get the ingredients out to make a muesli bar slice. Zoe helps me add everything to the bowl and stir it. I have what I think is an amazing idea to add melted chocolate to the slice, and the smells coming from our kitchen are divine! We pop it into the oven, and while it's cooking, I usher her into the lounge to choose a movie.

She takes her place on the couch—she's a bit like Sheldon from the *Big Bang Theory* and won't let anyone else sit in her spot. I put the disc in and get it started. I go back to the kitchen to make a hot drink and check on the slice. So far, so good.

I curl up on the couch and start reading, the movie playing in the background.

Do you ever find yourself getting sucked into children's movies? I do. I find myself chuckling along to the jokes that are put in there specifically for the parents.

I don't even think I got through a paragraph this time. The book is sitting next to me, and I'm enthralled in the movie that I've seen at least a dozen times already. How do they do that to us?

About halfway through the movie, I get a whiff of something. Something I can't quite put my finger on. I get up to investigate, and that's when it hits me. The muesli bar slice! Talk about baby brain!

I waddle as fast as I can into the kitchen and fling the oven door open. A billow of smoke wafts into my face and surrounds me. I swipe my hands in front of me, trying to wave the thick blackness from my vision. I bend down to retrieve the slice—if you can still call it that. It now resembles more of a black brick.

I take it to the back door and leave it to sit on the concrete outside, too afraid to leave it inside in case it melts something. I try and wave the smoke out the door with me, but it's too late and the smoke alarm starts blaring.

Zoe runs out, her hands clutched over her ears. "It's too loud, Mummy!" she cries out, coughing on the smoke she's inhaling.

"Come outside!" I yell over the noise. I drag a chair over to the offending alarm and on the third attempt I manage to get my cumbersome body up onto the chair so I can switch the blasted thing off.

But do you think I can find the switch? I end up ripping the whole thing off the ceiling, twisting and poking, trying to find the damn button to silence the high-pitched screeching. The sound is deafening. I don't know quite how I did it, but somehow, I make it stop. We may need to buy a new alarm…

Frazzled and Frumpy

My ears are ringing, and I'm panting with the effort it took. The smoke appears to have dissipated, and there is a black coating on the kitchen ceiling. I look outside to see Zoe poking a stick at the black brick on the path.

I slump down on the step outside, my head in my hands. I was really looking forward to that slice. I can't even recreate it because we used the last of our ingredients.

Calamity Jayne strikes again.

Knowledge

Did you know that when you turn five, you suddenly become all knowledgeable? No? I didn't either.

Since starting school, Ellie thinks she is the expert on all things, including, but not limited to, my driving.

That's right, I now have my very own backseat driver. Two, in fact, as Zoe has decided to jump on that bandwagon too. Aren't I lucky?

Apparently, Ellie turning five means that I no longer have the ability to know where I'm going or how to get there, nor do I know that I need to use my indicator while turning, or even that I am required to stop at a stop sign. I am also unable to differentiate between the different light colours on the traffic lights and need constant reminding.

"Mum! The light is red! That means you have to stop!" Zoe yells, holding her hands out in front of her, her fingers spread wide.

"I do realise that, sweetheart, but I'm not meant to just stop in the middle of the road, I actually have to keep going until I get up to the lights," I say.

"No! You have to stop!"

"Oh, I'm sorry. Do you have your license? Because last time I checked, you didn't. I've been driving for longer than you've been alive. I think I know the road rules a little better than you do," I huff sarcastically. This is not the first time today that I have been told what to do whilst driving. There is only so much you can handle.

"Do you even know where you're going, Mum?" Ellie pipes up.

I glance at her in the rearview mirror, my eyes narrowed. "Yes," I seethe.

"Why are you going this way? It's back that way." She points behind her.

I take a deep breath. *They're just children,* I remind myself.

"No. Remember, I said we were going to go to the library before going home. This is the way to the library."

"Are you sure?"

"Yes, I'm sure!" My fingers grip the steering wheel tighter. Sometimes I wonder why I bother taking them places. I force myself to take a deep, calming breath. My nostrils are assaulted with a godawful smell. "Oh gross! Who did that?" I ask, holding the back of my hand to my nose.

Zoe giggles. "It was me!" she sings gleefully.

I honestly have no idea how such fowl smells can come from a bottom so tiny. Even Devon's aren't as bad, and he's a teenage boy!

I hit the button on the door to open the windows and let some fresh air into the car, but it is inescapable. The smell lingers the entire trip to the library. I park the car and reluctantly wind the windows back up, not wanting to trap the smell inside, but not wanting to leave the car open for anyone to take—not that anyone would want to steal our car; it's in a constant state of filth; chip packets, odd socks, discarded jerseys, pieces of paper, lids from pens that are nowhere to be found, you name it, it's somewhere in there.

I climb out of the car and open Zoe's door to unbuckle her, and I am greeted with a smelly foot in my face. She giggles hysterically as she waves them about in front of me. Once again, she hasn't worn socks in her shoes and has decided that taking her shoes off on the way to the library is the best idea. No wonder the car was filled with such a horrible stench.

"Zoe, stop it. Put your shoes back on please, you can't go into the library with bare feet." I stand, hands on hips, tapping my foot as I wait. She takes her time climbing out of her car seat, wiggling her bottom as she bends down to retrieve her shoes, giggling the whole time. Oh, it's a great joke.

"Zooooeeee!" Ellie whines. "Hurry up! I want to choose some books!"

"I *am* hurrying!" Zoe yells, a scowl furrowing her brows as she finishes sliding both feet into the opposite shoes. I don't even bother to correct her this time.

We make it through the doors and the girls take off, running through to the children's section. It doesn't matter how many times I tell them a library is a quiet place, they will always run, and laugh loudly while they call across the room to each other, "Look at this book!"

Frazzled and Frumpy

I guess I should just be thankful they have adopted my love of reading. There's nothing quite like escaping inside a book for a few hours.

I settle on the couch by the picture books and pull out my book from home, hoping to sneak in a few minutes of reading time while they peruse the shelves. Of course, like the vultures that they are, they spy me having some 'me' time and come barrelling over, attempting to climb onto my almost non-existent lap. "Can you read this?" they ask.

I remind myself that they're only young, and I should embrace this time with them and not wish it away. I put my book back into my bag and manoeuvre myself into a better position so they can both see the book. Ellie snuggles into my side and rests her head on my chest, one hand idly rubbing my belly, while Zoe lies across both of our laps.

Sometimes it's nice to just take a break and enjoy the moment. I think, as parents, we put too much pressure on ourselves to make sure that our kids have the best of everything and are kept busy, but really, it's the simple things that are remembered fondly. Some of my favourite memories are of my sister and I snuggled up in our beds, eating supper of ice cream sundaes with chocolate sprinkles, while Gran read to us. We got to hear about *Tick-Tock* the horse, and Enid Blyton's *naughtiest girl in school, the children of cherry tree farm* and *Mr Pink Whistle*. Our imaginations would take flight as we listened to the soothing tones of her voice, and I'd like my children to experience that too. I guess that's why I made sure to read to them from early on.

I'm pretty lucky really. All three of my children love to read. I hope it stays with them as it has me.

Everyone's a Comedian

"Ellie, tell Mum and Dad the joke we practiced," Devon says with a grin, as we settle around the table for dinner. He had come home from school in a particularly good mood today and spent some time entertaining the girls for me while I prepared our meal.

"Okay. Knock knock," says Ellie.

"Who's there?"

"Interrupting cow,"

"Interrupting c—"

"MOOOOOO!" she interrupts in a fit of giggles. Zoe thinks it's hilarious and throws her head back in a hearty belly laugh.

I chuckle. "That *is* very funny, Ellie. Good job."

"I have a joke too!" Zoe adds in between giggles.

"Okay, sweetheart, what's your joke?"

She takes a deep breath, looking around the table as if preparing herself. "Knock knock."

"Who's there?" we all chorus.

"The interrupting cow." She is already sniggering before she gets the rest of the joke out.

Hubby and I exchange a smile. "The interrupting cow who?" I ask.

She gathers another deep breath. "MOOOOOOOO!" she yells and somehow continues to giggle at the same time. Her delivery alone is so comical that we all begin laughing along with her.

"I have another joke! Knock knock," she says, grinning at Ellie.

"Who's there?"

"Poop!" She covers her mouth with her hand, trying to contain her laughter.

"Poop who?" Ellie chortles.

"There's poop on your head!" She bursts into hysterics.

I don't think she quite understands the way a knock knock joke works. I turn my attention to Devon. "Go on then, joke master. What've you got?"

"Alright. You ready? Why did the chicken cross the road?" I look at him sceptically. I know there is going to be more to this than the old joke from my childhood.

"I don't know, why?"

"To get to the idiot's house." He smirks. "Knock knock."

I fold my arms across my chest. *And here it is.* "Who's there?"

"The chicken." He quirks an eyebrow at me, daring me to say something.

"Ha ha ha ha." I force out sarcastically with a slow clap. Yes, I stoop to that level sometimes. Hubby coughs to hide his amusement, and the girls are too caught up in their poop jokes to even notice.

"Mum, staring competition!" Devon yells, bracing his hands against the table and narrowing his eyes at me.

Frazzled and Frumpy

I turn my gaze to him and ever so slowly flare my nostrils. I've got this in the bag! He purses his lips, and I can tell he's trying hard not to break. I flare them again—in, out, in, out.

He breaks, a whimper of a laugh coming out as he clamps his mouth closed.

"And that's how it's done, Son!" I say, doing an imaginary mic drop.

"Best outta three!" he says, a huge grin on his face. I love these moments. They're few and far between, so I treasure them. It can change in a split second. Teenagers can be so moody!

He turns his head away from me, then counts, "One, two, three, GO!" He spins his head around, flicking his hair across his face in a Bieberesque way. I can tell he's already blown it. I barely even have to move, just a waggle of my eyebrow and it's all over. He tries to stop it, but the force is too strong, and he chokes out a laugh. "Not fair! How do you not laugh?" he asks.

"Years of practice," I say.

"Many, many years," hubby adds in, winking at me.

I nod in acceptance before pointing my fork in his direction. "Still not as many as you, though." I say it cockily, thinking I've won, but the victory is short-lived.

"Is Daddy *older* than you?" Ellie asks, a look of utter shock on her face. And just like that, the wind is let out of my sails. They always know how to make you feel so good about yourself.

Frazzled and Frumpy

CRUNCH

I'm too busy rubbing a hand over my face, wondering if I need to try a new anti-wrinkle cream, to register the noise coming from my side.

CRUNCH

I hear it this time, and when I turn to see where it's coming from, I see Zoe chomping on her chicken bone!

"Zoe, stop! You're not meant to eat the bone, sweetheart." I hold a hand under her chin, catching the remnants as she spits them out.

"You said I had to eat everything!" she cries.

"Yes. Yes I did. Sorry, sweetheart, I meant you had to eat all the *food* on your plate, not the bones as well." I shake my head, worry creasing my brow.

"She'll be fine," hubby says.

"But it's chicken bone. Isn't that like, really bad to eat? Ya know, splinters and such?" I ask quietly so as not to worry the children.

"I'm sure she didn't eat much of it. She'll be fine."

"You think?" I ask, studying the handful of chewed up bone I'm holding.

"Remember when she swallowed that magnetic ball? She was alright then. And when she shoved a pea up her nose? These things have a way of working their way out of the body. Stop worrying."

"Okay." I sigh. I might just keep an eye on her anyway.

Waste not Want not

I love that Zoe has finally got herself into a good sleeping pattern. What I don't love, is that my bladder hasn't picked up on that. Without fail, every morning at 5AM, I awake with that feeling of urgency. In fact, sometimes the urgency can be so strong that it invades my dreams. You know what I'm talking about. Those dreams where you're busting for the loo and then you finally find one and feel that sweet release. The ones that feel so real that when you wake up, you suddenly panic that you did, in fact, pee yourself. We've all had them. We've all had to surreptitiously pat ourselves down to be sure.

Today is no different. I am rushing about the house, desperately seeking the toilet but it keeps shifting from room to room. My legs are crossed as I half run, half gallop. Finally, the toilet appears in a closet, and I almost burst into tears at the sight. I race towards it, unbuttoning my pants as I go. I hover over the seat, ready to drop my pants and sit in one fluid motion. I feel the cool porcelain on my skin as I sit down and the relief is instant, but something in the back of my mind is telling me to stop.

I wake up. The dream felt much too real. I snake my hands down my body to my bottom. I gingerly pat myself and the surrounding mattress down. Phew! No wet patch! However, that urgency has reared its ugly head. Not a good time to be hugely pregnant with swollen feet.

I swing my legs over the edge of the bed and using the momentum I manage to get myself up in one go. Albeit too fast, as I'm now seeing white spots in my vision. Not a good sign. I reach out for the windowsill to steady myself, one leg crossed in front of the other as I try to keep from having yet another accident.

There's no time for a dressing gown and slippers. I ease my way to the bathroom, my legs firmly held together as I go, leaving my feet mere inches to step each time. It's not easy, but I manage to get there, tiny step by tiny step. Now, I don't know if you've ever been so busting that you don't actually know how you will get your pants down without peeing yourself, but I have. It takes a lot of skill, I can tell you! I thank God I'm not wearing jeans right now!

I hobble in as fast as my legs will allow. Positioning myself as close to the toilet as humanly possible, I hitch my nightie up around my waist, hook my fingers in the sides of my knickers an taking a deep breath, I yank them down at the same time as I lower my body.

That doesn't feel right.

Oh God!

Oh God, no! No, no, no, no!

The lid is down! Who leaves the lid down?!

My pee had already started coming out before I'd even settled myself and there's no stopping it now that it's started. I stare in horror at my feet, watching the puddle of pee pool around them as it flows like a waterfall from where I'm sitting. Why did I have that extra cup of tea before bed? I admonish myself.

This is a new low for me.

I am literally sitting in my own pee. Ew.

I don't even know where to begin to clean this mess up. I stand up, feeling the liquid dribble down the backs of my legs. There is too much to mop up with toilet paper, but to get to the cloths I would need to step out of the puddle and traipse it across the room. What a predicament I've gotten myself into.

I grab a wad of toilet paper and clean myself up as best as I can, then carefully drop strips on the floor in front of the puddle. I cautiously lift one foot and step forward. I place another sheet of paper on the floor and lift the other foot. I continue this until I have reached the bathroom door. I pull the door open and with my now dry feet, I step into the laundry to retrieve my cleaning rags and some disinfectant.

On my hands and knees, I slowly retrace my steps, wiping up my mess. I throw the soiled rags in the trash and fill a bucket with hot water and disinfectant. Who mops floors at five in the morning, I hear you ask? This girl, that's who.

The floors are now sparkling, and the bathroom smells clean and fresh. I, on the other hand, look like I've been dragged backwards through a hedge. My bed hair is swept to one side, my nightie is twisted and hitched high, and I have that distinct smell of pee emanating from me. So hot.

Frazzled and Frumpy

I peel my nightie off and chuck it in the sink to soak, then step into the shower to clean myself off.

When I emerge, all clean and smelling of blueberries, everyone is already up and about. Hubby has got the girls started on breakfast and is making himself a coffee.

"You're up early," he says.

"Yeah, baby bladder." I motion to my stomach and leave it at that. I head to the bedroom to get dressed. My phone chirps at me and I find a message from Carla asking if we want to do dinner tonight. With this baby due in mere weeks, I know this is probably the last time we'll be able to do so for a while, so I quickly type out a confirmation reply.

Sounds good! Will be good to catch up. Shall I bring dessert?

There really is no need for me to even ask, it's almost become a ritual for our dinners that I try to wow them with a new dessert recipe, and it just so happens there is one I've been dying to try out. Chocolate Caramel Tart. Doesn't it sound divine?

I put the phone down and forage around my drawers for something to wear. Hubby comes in with a cup of tea for me. "What are you grinning about?" he asks.

"Hmm? Oh, Carla just invited us for dinner tonight. I thought I'd make that Chocolate Pie I showed you the other day." I raise one eyebrow at him, knowing he can't resist a good dessert.

"Chocolate Pie, eh? Sounds amazing." He wraps his arms around my waist (well, that general area) and kisses my forehead. "I've got to get to work, but do you need me to pick anything up on my way home?"

"Mmm, no I don't think so. I'll have to go to the shop anyway."

"Okay, have fun making the pie." He grins, giving me another kiss. "Love you."

"Love you too. Have a good day," I call out as he disappears through the door.

Before we get stuck into making the pie, Zoe and I head into town to do a few jobs after dropping Ellie and Devon off at school. We go to the supermarket first to pick up the rest of the ingredients that we need.

Zoe carries the list and I hold the basket. Chocolate, butter, biscuits. She ticks them each off the list as we grab them. We even manage to make it out without a tantrum. I am suitably impressed.

The next stop is the recycling depot. I had completely forgotten to put the bin out this week, and it was starting to overflow, so Zoe and I had gathered some of the larger things to drop off, as well as a few of their old toys.

The children are constantly being given toys, either by older cousins or friends' children. Thus, their room is an absolute pigsty! So, before we left for school, I made each one choose a couple of toys to donate, and while they were at it, I had them find any broken toys to go in the bin.

"I want to keep my doll," Zoe had said.

"I know. I'm not going to throw out the toys you want, just the broken ones, or ones that you don't play with anymore."

"Okay, you can throw out my cashed redester. The key is missing."

"Your what?"

She sighed in an exaggerated manner. "My cashed redester."

"Ummm?"

In a loud, slow voice, sounding out every syllable, "Cashed Re-des-ter!"

"Cash register?"

"Yes! My cashed redester."

As you can see, that took quite some time, but we got there in the end.

Anywho, as we are leaving the recycling depot, Zoe pipes up from the backseat, "Do you know what the parsons bin is for?"

"I'm not sure, honey. What's it for?" I have no idea what she is talking about at this point, but I'm sure I can figure it out from her answer.

"It's for if you don't like your husbands," she says matter-of-factly.

"Wait, what? The what bin?" I ask again, paying closer attention to what she is saying.

"The parsons bin!"

"The purple bin?"

"No! The parsons bin!"

"The person bin?"

"Yes! It's for when you don't want your husbands anymore."

"So, you throw your husband in the bin?"

"Yeah. If you don't like them anymore."

I glance in the rear vision mirror to meet her eyes. She is looking at me with the most serious expression on her face. I try to stifle the laugh that wants to erupt.

"And who told you that?" I ask, thinking that my father had been making up stories again.

"No-one. I just know."

The things they come up with! You have to wonder where they get these ideas, sometimes.

Chocolatey Goodness

"MmmBop, doing up my shoe, bop!" I sing while I help Zoe put her apron on. What? You don't make up your own lyrics to entertain your children? Devon and I have got it down to a fine art now. My favourite is his version of *Blow a Kiss,* where he belts out "Fergus! Fire a gun." Makes way more sense than the actual lyrics if you ask me. And who doesn't love a bit of Hanson in the morning? You can belittle me all you want, but that song makes me happy. I will not apologise for my happiness. (Insert poking-out-tongue emoji here.)

Zoe giggles. "You're funny, Mummy."

"Am I?" I shimmy my shoulders awkwardly at her. "Dance with me!"

She doesn't need any convincing. Her hips start wiggling to the beat, while her head nods side-to-side with an entirely different one. We boogie around the kitchen, pulling bowls and teaspoons from the cupboards.

By the end of the song, we have everything that we need, all laid out on the bench. I empty the chocolate biscuits into the blender along with some melted butter. Zoe holds her hands to her ears, bracing herself for the noise. When it's done, we tip it into the pie dish and smooth it out before putting it in the fridge to set.

"Right, now for the fun part!" I announce. "The caramel!"

Zoe squeals in excitement.

I read through the instructions and start adding the ingredients to the saucepan. It's not the usual caramel mix that I make, so I watch it like a hawk. "It doesn't look very thick, does it?"

"It looks yummy!" Zoe says with gusto.

"It smells pretty good, too." I continue stirring, not wanting to leave it too long for fear it might burn. "I don't think it's going to thicken any more. Maybe it does that as it cools?" I give it another stir before taking it off the element. We bring the base back out from the fridge and carefully pour the hot caramel on top. Now that I'm pouring it, I can see that it really isn't thick at all. Not quite what I had envisioned.

"Can I taste it?" Zoe asks, her hands clasped together in a prayer-like position. She bounces up and down with unbridled enthusiasm.

"Okay, but just a little bit. It'll be our secret, okay?" I peer side-to-side as if making sure we're not being listened to. "Secret squirrel." I hold my pinkie finger up.

She wraps her pinkie around mine. "Secret squirrel," she says.

I grab a teaspoon and scrape it along the edge of the bowl before handing it to her.

"Mmmmmmm."

Frazzled and Frumpy

"That good, huh? I'd better have a taste too. You know, for quality control." I grin at her before popping a spoonful into my mouth. "Mmmmmm, you're right, it *is* good." It's velvety smooth with a hint of butterscotch. I think I may finally have my success story for the blog!

I quickly whisk the dish into the fridge to set. With it being so runny, I think it will need a little longer, so we clean up our mess while we wait.

When I check on it a few minutes later, the caramel is still very soft. Only the outer edges have started to firm up. I make the decision to put it in the freezer for a little bit, hoping that will help.

"Let's start on the chocolate topping." I grab a saucepan and add a little water before setting it on the stove with a glass bowl perched on top. We add the chocolate and butter and wait for it to begin melting.

Zoe licks her lips. "I want to be a baker just like you when I'm older," she says. "Then I can eat all the chocolate!" She cackles like a mini evil villain.

"I get to eat all the chocolate?" I gasp. "Nobody told me that!"

Zoe giggles. "No! You can't eat it all! It needs to go on the pudding, silly."

"Ooohhh yeah! The pudding. So, I get to eat all the pudding too?"

"No!" she yells. "It's for everyone!"

"But I thought you said I get to eat all the chocolate."

"No... I... didn't!" She is giggling so much that she can barely get the words out.

"Oh. Alright then. I *guess* I can share it with everyone." I sigh. "We can still have a wee taste though, right?" I ask her.

She nods. "Yes!"

"Secret squirrel?"

"Secret squirrel."

"That looks amazing!" Carla gasps, her eyes wide as she takes in the chocolate-crusted pie. "Did you make this?"

"You even need to ask?" I place a hand across my heart, feigning shock.

"Yeah, yeah. We all know you're a whiz in the kitchen." She winks at me.

"I helped!" Zoe pipes up, bounding toward me. "Mum gave me a spoon of caramel too," she announces proudly.

"Shhhhh! Secret squirrel, remember?" I whisper.

"Oh yeah. I forgot," she whispers back. "Just joking! We didn't have any caramel, eh, Mum?" She attempts to wink at me but really just blinks in an exaggerated way.

I run my hand over the top of her head, smoothing her hair out. "Good save, honey."

Frazzled and Frumpy

She beams up at me before running out to the lounge. "Pudding time, pudding time," she chants.

"Now, I'm not entirely sure if the caramel has set. It turns out I didn't read the instructions properly. I was meant to cook it a bit longer, and at a higher temperature…"

"True Calamity Jayne style." Carla chuckles.

"The proof is in the pudding," hubby says with raised brows. "Eh? You see what I did there?"

Adam claps him on the back. "Yeah, Fallon, we get it."

I ease the pie out of the dish and onto a plate. "So far, so good." I grab a sharp knife and plunge it into the centre. The chocolate topping is more of a ganache, so the knife slides through easily. I push the cake slice underneath the first piece and slowly lift. Caramel oozes out all over the plate.

"Okay, so maybe it wasn't quite the success I was hoping for," I say, disheartened.

"I don't know. It looks pretty damn good to me," hubby says encouragingly. He's always got my back.

The caramel is running out of the pie, and I have to work quickly. Carla hands me plate after plate as I slice each piece. I then grab a spoon to scoop up the caramel and make sure that everyone gets some. It ends up looking more like a chocolate pie with caramel drizzled over top.

"Oh God. This is so good!" Carla moans around her spoon. Everyone appears to be enjoying it, so I decide I'll take a pic for the blog anyways. I quickly flick a text to my sister, attaching the pic. **Jealous?** I add to the top of it.

She quickly responds with **I don't know. What is it?**

That doesn't exactly give me confidence. I take a bite all the same and, you know what? It may not be aesthetically pleasing, but damn! This pudding is amazing. Perhaps I should just change my whole blog name from *Calamity Jayne* to *Ugly Food That Tastes Good.*

Life is Hard Sometimes

"Devon, don't forget to do the dishwasher before you go out," I remind him for the third time this morning. He rolls his eyes at me and stomps past, his arms flailing by his side in typical teenage style. It's funny how they can be happy-go-lucky one moment, but then as soon as you ask them to do something, moody-teen rears its ugly head. It's not like he has that many jobs to do; keep his room tidy, empty the dishwasher, and clear the table after dinner. I don't think I'm asking too much. He, on the other hand, thinks I'm being unreasonable. Apparently, his friends don't have chores to do. What a load of rubbish.

I can hear him taking his frustrations out on the plates, clanging them together as he loads them back onto the shelf, so I sneak in to catch him out. He stomps back and forth taking one plate at a time, slamming it on top of the next one. He is completely oblivious to me leaning against the door frame with my arms folded.

I clear my throat. "Ahem. What did that plate ever do to you?" I ask, taking great pleasure in the fact that I have given him a fright.

"Nothing," he forces out through gritted teeth.

Frazzled and Frumpy

"Could have fooled me. You wanna try to be a bit more careful please? Otherwise, guess who will be buying new plates?"

He narrows his eyes at me, giving me what's known as 'evil eyes' or as I like to call it, 'the death glare'. He goes back to his job, exaggeratedly placing each plate carefully on the pile.

"You do realise you could make this a lot easier on yourself, by taking the whole pile at once, instead of one at a time, right?"

He mutters something under his breath that I can't quite catch. I'm not bothered, he can call me what he likes, as long as he gets his jobs done.

It's such a hard life being a teen, isn't it? All those pesky hormones flying around your body, so you wind up feeling frustrated for no reason. Not to mention all the peer pressure. I don't know about you, but I feel like things were simpler when we were kids. Sure, there was always that one kid who had the latest of everything, but the rest of us just made do with what we had, and we were happy to. We were lucky if we had a Nintendo or Sega Master System for the whole family to share. Now it seems that all the kids have their own game consoles, TV's, and of course, the one thing they can't seem to live without—a cell phone. Some of these kids even have fancier phones than I do! Now that's just not right. Devon is a klutz at the best of times. There is no way I would spend that kind of money on something he will drop within five minutes of owning. I believe he has been through more phones in the last two years than I have had over my entire adult life.

Frazzled and Frumpy

So, yes. I will make sure he does his three chores and does them properly. If he wants to have all these gadgets, then it's only fair he helps out around the house. Earns his keep, so to speak. How else am I going to prepare him for the real world?

I leave him muttering to himself and go to check on the girls. Zoe hasn't moved since I turned the TV on, but Ellie hasn't made it out of bed yet. I go to investigate.

She's lying on her bed, staring intently at the Lego alarm clock that she had made the day before.

"What's wrong?" I ask, kneeling on the floor beside her. I brush a wayward strand of hair behind her ear.

"I don't think my alarm clock works." She sighs, her beautiful hazel eyes filling with tears.

"Did it not ring?" I ask, stroking her cheek. I don't have the heart to tell her that it's not likely to ring at all.

"No," she whispers, not taking her eyes away from the clock. She looks so sad that I feel my own eyes begin to mist.

"Aww, honey. I'm sorry that it didn't work. Maybe we could get you one at the store. One that has batteries, so we know it will work. What do you think?"

She sniffs. "Okay."

"Okay." I kiss her forehead. "Come and get some breakfast, and then we can get ready to go." I spread my hands out on her mattress, needing the extra leverage to push up to my feet. It's getting harder and harder to move around with this bump. I swear baby has dropped even lower overnight and I seem to have developed an even wider waddle, almost as if I've been riding horseback. I have a feeling this baby is going to make an appearance sooner rather than later.

Devon decides to catch a ride with us to the store so he can meet up with his friends. As soon as the car has stopped, he gets out and rushes away. Obviously, it's too embarrassing to be seen with your mother.

I attempt to hold both the girls' hands as we make our way across the parking lot. Zoe tries to wriggle free the entire time, meaning that I have to have a Vulcan-like grip on her. This, of course, makes her squirm even more.

"Mum!" she whines. "Let me go!"

"Zoe, we've been over this a hundred times before. This is a busy carpark. You are too little for the cars to see you. You need to hold my hand until we are in the store."

"I can do it myself!" She breaks free and makes a mad dash across the main driveway in front of the store. A car is coming straight for her, and I lunge forward, grasping her wrist and yanking her backwards in the nick of time.

Frazzled and Frumpy

"Zoe, don't do that to me! You nearly got hit by a car!" I yell. My heart is beating at hyper speed and tears have started pooling in my eyes at the thought of losing my daughter.

"Mum! You hurted me!" she cries, her face twisted in anger. Admittedly, I probably used more force than necessary, but when you see a car headed straight for your child, adrenalin kicks in and you just act.

I get down to her level. "I'm sorry that I hurt you. I just... I needed to keep you safe," I choke the words out, trying desperately not to cry. "You really scared me."

She must see the anguish in my eyes, because she wraps her arms around my neck and nuzzles in. "Sorry, Mummy."

I cling to her, pulling Ellie in to my other side. I don't know what I would do if anything happened to them.

We stay in that position for a few more minutes. The girls have started fidgeting, and I know it's time to let go. My legs have seized slightly, and it takes a great effort to stand up. I grab both of their hands again and take one wobbly step after another.

We head straight for the aisle with the clocks to select an alarm clock for their room. The girls bound down the aisle, giggling and pointing out all the different kinds. I can't say I've ever been as excited as they appear to be whilst buying a clock, but each to their own.

Frazzled and Frumpy

They settle on a pink clock with a ballerina on it. Taking turns to carry it, we make our way down various other aisles, perusing the shelves. Nothing like a bit of browsing.

"Oh cool! Mum, look! Surfboards!" Ellie exclaims excitedly. I hang my head in shame. Those are not surfboards. They are ironing boards. Clearly, I am not the domestic goddess I thought I was if my daughter doesn't even know the difference between a surfboard and an ironing board.

I decide to humour her anyways. "Yeah, they are pretty cool, eh?" I notice another woman standing nearby, sniggering. "I don't have the heart to tell her," I say, shrugging. She laughs.

"Don't worry, I don't think my kids would know either!"

"Well, I mean, really. Who irons these days?" We both laugh. It's always nice to meet another kindred spirit.

Not Enough

When hubby gets home at lunch time, I am sitting on the floor, my legs spread wide, folding pamphlets.

"Stop what you're doing," he says, resting his hands on my shoulders as he bends down to kiss me. "That is Devon's job, not yours."

"I know. He's still out with his friends, and there are a lot of them, so I thought I'd give him a hand."

"You already do enough around here without taking on his job. Take a break."

"I will soon, just let me finish this pile." I smile up at him before a twinge in my back turns it into a wince.

"You're overdoing it." He tuts. "I'm going to put the jug on, I want you on that couch with your feet up when I come back through." He looks at me with a mix of worry and love. It's sweet the way he dotes on me.

"Yes, Sir." I salute him, poking my tongue out at the same time. He chuckles as he walks away. I turn back to my pile and continue folding the last few. I've already done a third of them, he should be happy with that. Pushing the box away, I bring my legs back together, leaning my upper body backwards to allow for my belly. I roll slightly to the side so I can fold my legs under me, but I've been sitting too long and my body won't co-operate. I try rolling to the other side, and this time I am able to get into a better position. I swing my arm across me, bracing it on the floor in front of me so that I land on all fours. My breath puffs out in quick succession as I crawl towards the couch to use for leverage. It should *not* be this hard!

"You alright there?" hubby asks, sauntering back into the lounge as if he doesn't have a care in the world. I'd like to see him try to carry around an extra 20kg and see how he feels!

"I'm fine," I grumble, taking my frustrations out on him even though I know it's not his fault that I'm uncomfortable. I chose to get down on the hard floor and sit at an awkward angle for the last half an hour.

"Here, let me help." His arms slip under my armpits and he hoists me up to my feet, guiding me to the couch. "Now, sit down and don't move. I'll make you a cup of tea."

"Thanks," I mutter, managing a tight smile. It really does feel good to be back on something soft. So good that I'm questioning my sanity for getting down on the floor in the first place.

I let out a deep breath and rest my head on the cushions behind me, relishing in the cushiness. *I'll just close my eyes for a minute...*

"Muuuuuuuuummmm?" The long whine breaks through to my subconscious, and I blink my eyes open. "Whatcha doing?" Zoe asks, climbing onto my ever-diminishing lap.

"Hmmm? Um, nothing, just resting my eyes. What are you doing?" I notice the cup of tea sitting on the table in front of me, a waft of steam rising up letting me know I haven't been asleep for long. I rub my eyes, giving Zoe a sleepy smile.

"Ellie won't play with me." She frowns and tries to fold her arms but ends up hugging herself instead. "She said she's not my friend anymore." Her voice is so tiny and filled with hurt. She has tears in her eyes, and I just want to wrap her up in my arms.

"Oh, honey. I'm sure she didn't mean that."

"She did. She said she is leaving." She pauses, gathering her breath. "I don't want her to leave!" She can't contain her tears any longer as they spill over her long lashes. I pull her in tight, kissing the top of her head.

"She's not leaving."

"Yes, she is."

"No, she's not. I won't let her. I promise." I shift her from my lap and after several attempts, I get up from the couch. "Ellie?" I say, hobbling over to their room. I find her sitting on the floor with her school bag in her lap while she piles in a few toys and some knickers. She has a scowl on her face. "Ellie, what're you doing?"

"I'm running away!" she cries.

"Why?"

"Because. Zoe ripped my picture!"

"I'm sure she didn't do it on purpose."

"Yes, she did!"

"No, I didn't!" Zoe yells from the lounge. "It was a accident!"

"No, it wasn't!"

Frazzled and Frumpy

"Alright, that's enough. Zoe, come in here please." I wait for her to join us, then I take them both by the hand. "Look at each other. You are sisters, and you love each other," I say. "Zoe, I know it was an accident, but you need to say sorry to Ellie."

"Sorry, Ellie," she says, the corners of her mouth twitching.

"Ellie, you need to apologise for telling her you didn't want to be her friend."

"Sorry, Zoe."

"Now, give each other a kiss and a cuddle." They giggle but do so. "See? Isn't that better?" They nod.

"Zoe, do you want to play Mummy and baby?" Ellie asks, and just like that, they are back to being best friends.

I go back to my cup of tea but can't help but notice the pile of washing sitting in the corner. I drag it over to the couch with me and begin folding.

"I thought I told you to rest," hubby says, coming in from outside.

"I'm still resting, I'm just folding washing at the same time," I say. "What have you been up to?"

"I ah, was putting something together in the shed," he says cryptically.

"Okay, do I get to see it?"

"Yeah, of course. I made it for you." He smiles and the corners of his eyes crinkle. Have I mentioned how beautiful his smile is? "Wait here, I'll bring it in."

I take a sip of my tea, wondering what it could be.

"Ta-dah!" he says, walking through the door with a bookshelf! "An old staircase came in at work, solid

Rimu, so I grabbed it and made this for you. I know you've had your eyes on those ones in the store, but I hope you like it."

My mouth gapes open. "You made this?" I ask in wonder.

"Yeah." He grins and runs his hand through his hair. "I know you've got a stack of books with nowhere to put them, so…"

"It's beautiful," I whisper, running my hand over the top of it. "It's so rustic, I love it!" I tackle him, throwing my arms around his neck. "Thank you," I say breathlessly. "I love you."

"I love you, too." He kisses my nose. "Where do you want me to put it?"

"Ummm." I spin around, looking for the perfect spot. "How about over there?" I point to a spot just beside our bedroom door.

"Perfect." He lifts it with ease and carries it to its new home. I quickly go into the bedroom to grab my books and start loading them onto the shelves. I then take one of our wedding photos and sit it on top.

Standing back to admire it, I say, "It's perfect. Thank you." I am blown away with his thoughtfulness.

"There's still some wood leftover. I thought maybe I could make you another one for the next lot of books you collect. If you want."

"Are you kidding? I would love that!" I fan my hands in front of my face. "You're gonna make me cry!"

He chuckles. "I didn't mean to make you cry. I can just make something else…"

"Don't you dare! You've said it now, you have to follow through." I wipe my fingers under my eyes, discarding any tears.

"Okay, okay," he says, holding his hands up in surrender. "Slave driver," he adds as he walks past me with a smirk on his face.

"Check it out! I got a laser!" Devon barges through the door brandishing a small metal tube. "It shoots like really far away."

"I hope you mean a laser pointer and not an actual laser."

"Duh, of course, Mum." He rolls his eyes. "Like I'd get an actual laser." He pushes a button, and a green dot starts dancing along the wall.

"And what exactly do you need that for?" I ask, watching the tiny light.

"So I can point at stuff that's far away."

I raise my brow at him and clear my throat. "You do realise you have these things called fingers? They're on your hand and they too can be used for pointing at things."

He forces out a sarcastic laugh. "It's not as fun to do that, though." He points his finger with a lame look on his face. "I mean look at it!" He assumes an entirely different stance, acting like he's the bee's knees. "It can reach the neighbours roof!"

"I'm sure it can. You know, you can point at the neighbour's roof with your finger too. Or you could use your words and tell people what it is that you're looking it."

"Gah, you just don't get it!" He storms off to his room. "Oh man! Pamphlets!" He draws the word out in a whine.

"You knew you had them to do. I already folded some for you."

"But there's so many! I can't get them all folded!" He throws his hands in the air in exasperation.

"Um, yeah you can. It didn't take me long to fold that lot." I point (using my fingers) at the box by his door.

"But you're faster than me. It's going to take me all night!"

"Devon, it's your job. You wanted to have a job to earn money so you could buy these useless contraptions you have an affinity for. Having a job means you actually have to do some work."

"It's kind of in the title. It's a job," hubby says as he joins us. "Nice laser, by the way." He smirks.

Devon either ignores the tone of his voice or doesn't notice, because he jumps into yet another spiel about how fantastic his laser is. I leave them to their discussion and start preparing dinner. I'm feeling rather tired today, so a simple dish of baked potatoes and cheese sauce will do. Nice and easy, with minimal dishes. Just the kind of meal I like!

While the potatoes are cooking, I wash up the dishes from the rest of the day so I can relax after dinner. I feel as though I've been on my feet all day. My back is protesting, and I swear my feet have swollen even more. Perhaps hubby had a point. Maybe I am doing too much. My due date is nearly upon us, I suppose at some point I have to give in and let the others help out some.

Once everything is ready, I set the placemats on the table and call out to everyone. "Dinner is ready!" I ladle the cheese sauce over the piping-hot potatoes and top with some extra cheese before carrying them out to the table.

Ellie takes one look at her plate and screws her nose up. "Just cheese?" she asks in disgust. "If I was a Mum, I'd do more than that."

Did she actually just say that to me? I stand with my mouth agape, unable to muster a response.

Hubby comes to my rescue. "Excuse me, Miss. There is no need to speak to your mother that way. She has worked very hard today *and* made us a lovely dinner. Now, you apologise."

"Sorry, Mum." She picks up her fork and pushes her food around her plate. I sit down and stare at my plate. I used to love it when Mum made meals like this. They were my favourite. Apparently, that's not good enough for my children, though.

"Mum?" Zoe says.

"Mmmm?" I barely even look up from my plate.

Frazzled and Frumpy

"I love you."

Awww.

"I love you too, sweetheart," I say. My pregnancy hormones are going into hyper drive right now, and tears spring to my eyes. They always know when I need to hear those three magic words. They may not always appreciate what I do, but at least I know they will always love me.

"I love you too, Mum," Ellie whispers and I reach out to rub her hand.

"It's okay, sweetheart. I know. I love you, too."

Ready or Not

I'm lying in bed, staring at the ceiling while hubby snores happily beside me. I'm not sure what woke me, but I can't get back to sleep. My mind has started questioning my entire existence, the meaning of life, and of course, where I put my keys, because what better time to do that, than half past three in the morning? It's as if my body has become used to waking at this time now. I really wish someone would tell it that it is a ridiculous time to be awake. Especially when you have three children to get up to in the morning. Not to mention all the dishes and mounds of washing. Is it just me, or is that never-ending when you have kids? Anyone else feel like they live in a laundromat? I mean, I get to the bottom of the pile, and then I walk past it five minutes later and it's over-flowing again! How does this happen? And why the hell am I thinking about it at *half past three in the morning*?!

I decide to get up and make myself a drink, maybe read or check up on Facebook. It's even harder to manoeuvre out of bed this time. Is it possible this baby has grown bigger again? I swear there is no more room in the inn. My skin is stretched as tight as it can go, and I really don't want to add any more stretch marks to the myriad I have already.

Frazzled and Frumpy

I hobble out the door, noting how uncomfortable I am. So much downwards pressure. Could it be? Is this why I'm awake at stupid o'clock? I rub my belly affectionately. "Are you coming to meet us today?" I whisper as I waddle to the kitchen.

While I wait for the jug to boil, I pop my head into each of the children's rooms, checking they still have their covers on. I then double-check that my hospital bag is ready and waiting by the door, where I've left it since the pee incident.

I grab a towel from the linen closet and drape it across the couch—just in case—before sitting down with my tea. I grab my phone and scroll through the notifications, the screen casting a glow across my face. I know it's probably not the best for my eyes, sitting in the dark staring at a bright screen, but I can't risk waking the kids.

"Everything okay?" hubby whispers, rubbing a hand through his hair, his bare feet padding softly towards me.

"Yeah, I just couldn't sleep. I think maybe this baby is going to join us soon. I'm okay though. You go back to bed." I smile up at him.

"You sure? I don't mind sitting up with you."

"No, don't be silly. No point in both of us being tired and cranky tomorrow. I'll wake you if anything happens."

"Okay." He draws the word out.

"I'm fine, really." I wave my hand, shooing him away. "Go and get some sleep."

He nods and reluctantly heads back to bed.

Frazzled and Frumpy

My tea is cool enough to drink now, so I hold it tightly in my hands, letting the heat warm them before taking a large gulp. There is something so soothing about a warm cup of tea. Maybe because it's another thing that reminds me of my grandmother. That woman is amazing. She is always so calm, and as I mentioned earlier, her voice could lull us to sleep when we were children. I don't think I've ever seen her angry or flustered. She just takes everything in her stride and keeps on going. It would be nice to be like that, to not have frustration bubbling just below the surface. Sometimes I feel like a teen again, where my emotions are overtaking my body. I guess I'm just an emotional person, but let's face it, we knew that already.

Thinking of my grandmother has had that calming effect on me, and I feel like I could go back to sleep now. I gulp down the last mouthful of tea before pushing myself up off the couch. I take two steps before warm liquid starts gushing down my legs and I am forced to clamp them together as I crab-walk to the bathroom. This time I know it's my waters. There's no mistaking it. Well, that's not entirely true. I remember when I was pregnant with Devon, my waters broke in a similar fashion, and I thought I was peeing myself! I tried so hard to stop it from coming out, but it wouldn't. That was when I realised what was happening.

Anyways, I make it to the bathroom and attempt to go to the toilet and clean myself up a bit, though this is not easy when you have a constant flow running down your legs. In the end, I give up and decide to jump in the shower. I let the hot water rain down on my lower back as I brace myself against the wall. This is it. We're meeting our baby today!

There is a gentle knock on the door, and hubby pokes his head in. "Everything okay?"

"Mmmhmm," I say, as the first contraction hits me full force. I hiss a breath through my teeth. "Shit that hurt!"

"What do you need?" He has already stepped into the bathroom and is offering me a large towel. I take a shaky step towards him, my legs feeling as though they may buckle beneath me. "Whoa there. Let me help you."

"I'm okay."

"Honey, let me help you." He wraps his arm around my back and takes my weight as I step out of the shower. The fluffy towel is instantly draped around me and he begins rubbing my lower back.

"Thanks," I manage to get out before another contraction hits. "I need... to call..."

"I'm on it. I'll call your mum, too." He moves towards the door, then quickly runs back to me, planting a kiss on my cheek. "I love you," he says, his face creased with worry.

"Love... you... too," I pant. Geez this baby is in a hurry! I don't know why that surprises me though, each of my babies have been birthed in a matter of hours. Devon took the longest, at around seven hours from start to finish. Zoe, however, was only four. I have a feeling this baby will be even quicker.

That thought alone both scares and excites me. I will actually get to see the beautiful face of the little person I have been carrying inside me for the last 38 weeks. How can I not be excited by that?

The pain, however. I had forgotten how strong those contractions can be, and *that* is what scares me. I know this is just the beginning and I still have more to come. I'm one of those people who don't like to use any pain relief during labour. That might sound crazy to some, but I like to experience the whole thing. I mean, we women have this amazing ability to create and carry life inside of us, and I think there is nothing more beautiful than being fully aware throughout. Being present. And the truth is, that pain? It all goes away the instant you see your baby. When you hold their warm little body in your arms, and they open their eyes and gaze up at you. When you finally get to meet that person you've already formed an unbreakable bond with, without even having laid eyes on them. That is when you truly feel like a mother and everything becomes real. That pain goes away, and you realise it was all worth it. Every last minute of it.

So, yeah. I'm scared shitless right now, but I know that I can do it. There's no going back now!

I manage to dry myself through the contractions and with a towel lodged between my legs, I don't my dressing gown and make the slow journey back to the bedroom to get something to put on. Hubby has made the calls and is in the kitchen preparing some food to take with us—I have a tendency to pass out after birthing our children, and this is something we thought might help.

Frazzled and Frumpy

"Are you okay? Do you want me to help you?" he asks, rushing to my side.

"I think… I'm… okay," I pant. "Just… getting… dressed." I shoo him away and shuffle on past. I can't be bothered finding clothes, so I pull on a nightie and some slippers. I hear my parents arrive as I slip my arms back into my dressing gown. Thank God they only live a few houses away. The children will be surprised to find them here in the morning, but it's better than waking them to go to the hospital.

"How are you feeling?" Mum asks as I join them.

"Sore."

"Not long now," she reminds me, smiling. I nod, unable to answer as yet another contraction rocks my body. Have you ever had a pain so strong that you find yourself moving, trying to get away from it, but you can't because it's *in* your body? That's what is happening.

"We… need… to go," I say. I can feel the baby wiggling down into my pelvis with each contraction, and I know it won't be long until I can't control the urge to push.

"Okay," hubby says, grabbing his keys. He turns to Mum and Dad. "Devon knows where everything is. Make sure he helps out with the girls."

"Don't worry, we know what we're doing." Mum smiles at him reassuringly. "Go."

He doesn't have to be told twice. He wraps one arm around me, guiding me to the door, while the other scoops up the hospital bag. He helps me into the car, closing the door and running around to the driver's side. Once we are on the road, he reaches over and grabs my hand, giving it a squeeze. "This is it, baby."

A Child is Born

When we arrive, I see that my midwife has already prepared the birthing pool. She and a nurse are standing by, ready to assist me in any way. Without hesitation, I strip off (an entire circus of people could be in this room right now, and I honestly wouldn't care at this point), and with the help of hubby, step into the warm water. It doesn't ease the pain, but it helps to relax me somewhat.

"How are we feeling?" the midwife asks.

I attempt a smile, but the contractions are coming too close together now and I end up grimacing. A whimper escapes my lips as the pressure on my stomach increases.

"They're only minutes apart now," hubby says. He rubs my back with one hand while the other is being squeezed within an inch of its life by my own.

"I... I donwanna... donwanna... doooooo!" I nearly double over as I try to get the words out. "I don't wanna do this anymore!" I cry, panting through the pain.

"You can do this. You know that means you're nearly there," my midwife soothes.

"You're doing great," hubby whispers in my ear, and I try hard to focus on his voice.

Frazzled and Frumpy

"I… need… to push! Aaaaaaarrrrrrghhhhhhh!" My body begins bearing down on its own. I no longer have control over it.

"Good girl, you're doing great!" the midwife says, standing behind me. "I can see the head already. One more big push!"

I gasp in a breath before my body takes over again and I feel my baby's head between my legs. I begin to pant, the exhaustion hitting me suddenly.

"You're doing great. We're nearly there. You're a natural. We've just got to get these shoulders out." The midwife climbs into the pool with me to help. "Little pushes, okay?"

"Uh-huh," I manage to grunt before I feel the need to begin pushing again. I have to fight my body so that I don't push too hard.

"I need you to spread your legs a bit more."

"I can't!"

"I need you to focus. The baby is stuck, so we need to help him get out. We're going to help you." She motions to hubby, "I'm going to need you to take her weight." She touches my back to let me know it's time. "Wrap your arms around his neck and let him help you." With great effort, I manage to get to my feet, and she somehow pushes my legs apart even more, so that I'm now in a yoga-like pose, with one leg scissored in front of the other. I can tell you right now, that is no easy feat. Trying to stand up and move around with a baby hanging between your legs is one of the scariest things ever.

Frazzled and Frumpy

"Okay, I need you to try and push again. Little pushes."

I couldn't stop it even if I tried. My body knows what it's doing after birthing three children already. I can feel wiggling and a burning sensation and then that amazing feeling of relief, as my baby comes rushing out in one go.

"Congratulations. You have a beautiful baby boy," my midwife says with a smile. Hubby helps to lower me back down to a seated position and then my little man is in my arms. He's not making a sound, just blinking slowly as his eyes adjust to his new surroundings.

"Hi," I murmur through my tears. "I'm your mummy." He stares into my eyes and I am instantly in love. "He's so beautiful," I whisper, not taking my eyes off him.

"He sure is. So are you," hubby says, kissing my forehead and gently stroking our son's head.

"Do we have a name?" the nurse asks. I'd forgotten she was even in the room.

"We do." I look up at hubby.

"Oliver. Oliver James," he says.

Frazzled and Frumpy

Propped up in bed, a sweet cup of tea and a sandwich on the table beside me, and baby Oliver in my arms, I feel like the luckiest woman on Earth. He is sleeping soundly, the whole birthing experience too much for his tiny body to handle, and I am enjoying a much-needed rest.

The midwife comes in and asks if she can take his measurements. I reluctantly agree, handing my little bundle over. I *do* want to know what he weighs. He doesn't seem as big as the others, which is surprising.

She strips him down, and places him on the scales. "He's a whopper!" she says with a laugh. "5.1kg!"

"Really?" I ask incredulously. "I was so sure he was smaller." I can't help but giggle. "I definitely didn't expect that. What's that in pounds?"

"Let me just check." She studies her chart. "11lb 3oz."

"Wow."

"Wow alright. You really are made for pushing out big babies," she says with a wink. "He's tall, too. 69cm."

"That'll be why he didn't look as big, he's longer and not so pudgy." I smile down at my little man who is now kicking his legs in the air, his face scrunched up.

"Nearly done," the midwife says, rubbing his tummy. She records all the measurements and dresses him again. "You ready to try feeding him?"

"Sure." I adjust my pillows and ease myself back up on the bed. I'm still sticky from the pool and haven't bothered to put clothes on yet, so the girls are hanging out in the open. I cradle him in my arms, and he latches on straight away. I look over to hubby who is starting to doze on the couch. "Babe?"

"Mmm? I'm awake," he mumbles.

"Go home and get some sleep. I'm okay here."

"No, no. I'm fine."

"You need to get some rest, and then you can bring the kids in later." I look down at the dark blue-grey eyes that are watching me. "We'll be fine, won't we?" I ask Oliver.

Oliver is a dream baby. He fell asleep shortly after his feed, allowing me time to eat something. They wouldn't let me have a shower until after lunch because of the passing out thing. So ,I caught up on some sleep while I had the chance.

The nurse brought in some more sweet tea and a cooked meal for lunch, which I happily devoured. My eyes kept flicking to the clock on the wall, patiently waiting until I was allowed to clean up. The nurse finally gave in and escorted me down the hall to the bathroom.

"Just push the button if you need me," she says, pulling the door closed behind her. I don't want to be away from Oliver too long, so I wash as quickly as I can. The warm water washes away all the sticky sweat that has been caked on my body, and I am beginning to feel more like myself again—albeit, tender.

I rummage through my bag and pull out a large tee and some trackies. Once dressed, I rake a hand through my hair and pull it up into a rough ponytail. A quick brush of my teeth and I am ready to face the world again.

Back in the room, Oliver stirs. I carefully pick him up and hold him close, humming. I grab a pillow for my back and sit in one of the chairs. My phone pings beside me and I see a message from hubby.

How's it going? You up to visitors? I have some little people who would like to meet their brother.

I smile and quickly type out a response.

Doing great. Just had a shower and feel good. Oliver would love to meet them too.

I put the phone back down and continue humming. Oliver snuffles and nestles into my chest making my heart melt even more. I can't help but inhale his new-baby scent as I plant kisses on his head. His fluffy hair is so soft and fine, that I find myself rubbing my cheek along the top of his head.

He bobs his head about, his mouth open, searching for a feed. I chuckle lightly. "Are you hungry again, little man?" I ask. I gently lay him across my body and prepare to feed him. This time he doesn't quite get on properly, and I let out a little yelp as he starts sucking on the tip of my nipple. I shove my little finger in the corner of his mouth to break the seal, though he does his best to hang on. I finally get him on correctly, but it's sore. I think there may be a blister.

"Knock, knock," hubby says softly, peering into the room. "You have visitors."

"Come in," I say, trying to conceal my pain. He opens the door and the girls come bounding in, followed by Devon and my parents. "Hi guys, you want to meet your baby brother?" I smile.

"Yeah," the girls say in unison. They both creep up to me and peer at the tiny bundle in my arms.

"What's he doing?" Zoe asks, her brow furrowed.

"He's drinking milk," Ellie says matter-of-factly. "That's how babies get their food, eh, Mum?"

"It sure is. You two did this when you were babies too."

"We did?" Zoe asks, her eyes wide.

"Yip." I nod.

Ellie reaches out and cautiously touches his finger. "He's so soft," she says.

"He is, isn't he? We have to be really careful with him. Nice, gentle hands, Zoe."

"Okay." She touches his cheek. "Can I pat him?" she asks.

"Well, I don't know if he'd like that right now. Maybe once he's finished having his lunch you could touch his hand."

"Okay."

Hubby clears his throat. "Zoe made you something." He hands me a clear plastic box with a very phallic-looking piece of playdough. It's a long strip, attached to a ball-shaped piece.

"It's a lollypop!" she says excitedly.

"That's beautiful, Zoe. Thank you."

I catch hubby's eye and he mouths *I know, right?*

Mum steps around the girls and gives me a kiss. "He's beautiful. Well done."

"Thanks, you can have a hold when he's finished." I beam up at her, a wave of emotion washing over me.

"What's wrong?" she asks, her face full of concern.

"Nothing," I whisper, reaching for her hand. I look around the room at my family, the people I love the most in this world and everything falls into perspective. I really am the luckiest woman in the world. I may not be the domestic goddess I wanted to be, or the entrepreneurial wizard, but damn it, I have a happy, healthy family. What more could I possibly ask for?

Frazzled and Frumpy

Acknowledgements

Firstly, I have to thank my family, without which, I would not have so many stories to tell! My wonderful children provide me with a lot of inspiration for these books.

My husband, for all of his patience as I sit at the computer for hours on end. And for being my rock. I'm so thankful that I have your support and that you encourage me to follow my dreams.

To my parents, for their encouragement and words of wisdom. Thank you for encouraging my love of reading which, in turn, allowed me to explore this amazing world of writing.

To my grandmother, for the wonderful memories I drew on throughout this story. For always being there for me when I need you.

To my friend and partner in crime, Petrina, for making sure that my writing is as good as it can be, and for picking up on any mistakes before I put it out there for the world to see. I couldn't do this without you!

Frazzled and Frumpy

To my incredible friends who let me bounce ideas off them and regale me with stories of their own that I can use. For always being there for me. For telling people to read my books. You guys are amazing, and I love you all.

To my amazing support crew on Facebook and all the bloggers who have reviewed and shared my stories! You guys rock my world! Thank you for all that you do, and for helping me to share Super Mum with the world.

And, of course, to the readers! Without you, there would be no book world. Thank you for taking the time to read my books. I hope you enjoy them as much as I enjoy writing them!

If you enjoyed reading Frazzled and Frumpy, I'd love if you could post a quick review on your favourite platform.

Thanks again!

Connect with me

http://www.staceybroadbent.weebly.com

https://www.facebook.com/StaceyBroadbentAuthor

Broadbent's Bookish Babes: https://goo.gl/FY9wQN

https://www.amazon.com/author/staceybroadbent

Goodreads: https://goo.gl/YJ6dXa

https://www.instagram.com/authorstaceybroadbent/

https://www.bookbub.com/authors/stacey-broadbent

https://vm.tiktok.com/ZSJBb5bhL/

Newsletter sign-up: http://eepurl.com/cULu_f

Other Books by Stacey Broadbent

Standalone
Never Judge a Book
Deep Heat

Super Mum series
Frazzled
Frazzled and Frumpy
Frazzled, Frumpy and Fabulous
Super Mum: the complete series

Flesh-eater series
Fear the Fever
Fight the Fever

Dark Sins Novellas
Sins of the Flesh
Mine

Hollywood Novels
Emma

Frazzled and Frumpy

A Step in Time series
Dancing through the Storm
Dancing in Circles
Dancing with Destiny
A Step in Time: the complete series

Short Stories and Poetry
Musings, Mournings, and Misadventures

Anthologies
The White Ribbon Collection
Scars to your Beautiful
Witching Hour: Vices and Virtues
Key to my Heart
A Touch of Inspiration
No Place like Home
Serendipity

Frazzled and Frumpy

Stacey resides in Ashburton, New Zealand with her husband and three children. She is a qualified proofreader, author, wife, mother, and self-proclaimed culinary goddess. When she's not busy writing or editing books, she enjoys reading and procrastinating on TikTok.

She absolutely loves hearing from readers, so please feel free to reach out via email, Instagram, or join her reader group, Broadbent's Bookish Babes. You can also sign up to her newsletter for up-to-date info on releases.

www.staceybroadbent.weebly.com